Up North
at the Cabin

by Marsha Wilson Chall
paintings by Steve Johnson

Lothrop, Lee & Shepard Books ◆ New York

First Edition   1   2   3   4   5   6   7   8   9   10

Library of Congress Cataloging in Publication Data
Chall, Marsha Wilson. Up north at the cabin / by Marsha Wilson Chall ; illustrated by Steve Johnson.
p.   cm. Summary: Summer vacation up north at the cabin provides memorable experiences with the water, the animals,
and other faces of nature. ISBN 0-688-09732-4. — ISBN 0-688-09733-2 (lib. bdg.)   [1. Nature—Fiction.   2. Vacations—Fiction.]
I. Johnson, Steve, 1960–   ill.   II. Title. PZ7.C3496Up   1992   [E]—dc20   91-30358   CIP   AC

Book and cover design by Lou Fancher

On the way up north to the cabin,

the sunshine sits in my lap all morning.

I know the way by heart:

past the big walleye statue on Lake Mille Lacs,

a few more miles to the Live Deer Park,

till all the trees are birch and pine

and houses are made from logs

that look like shiny pretzels.

Up north at the cabin,

I am a smart angler.

Grandpa tries pink spinners,

leeches, and dragonflies—

but I know what fish like.

I bait my hook with

peanut-butter-and-worm sandwiches,

then jig my line and wait.

Grandma serves my sunnies
with fried potatoes and corn-on-the-cob.
We eat at the long table on the screen porch,
sitting next to one another on the same side
so we can all watch the loons
dance down the sun.

Up north at the cabin,

I am a great gray dolphin.

The lake is my ocean.

From the dock I dive headfirst,

skimming over sand that swirls behind me.

Anchored to the bottom, upside down,

I am an acrobat in a perfect handstand.

Then rising in a sea of air-bubble balloons,

I float on a carpet of waves.

Up north at the cabin,

I am a fearless voyageur

guiding our canoe through the wilderness.

The river spills over rocks

and whispers to me—

Kawishiwee...Kawishiwee—

and rushes on to anywhere.

Like a house on stilts,

a bull moose stands in the shallows.

His chest heaves and rumbles,

mighty as a diesel engine.

He shakes his great head,

rocking branches of bone

as he bellows a warning.

"Ahead to the beaver dam!"
the voyageur commands.
On the portage trail,
we sling the canoe over our heads.
Its backbone to the sky,
we trudge along—
an armored beetle homeward bound.

Up north at the cabin,

I am a daredevil.

"Keep your knees bent," calls Uncle Roy.

I clutch the tow rope,

bobbing up and down in my yellow life vest.

The motor sputters softly, waiting.

My legs stiffen in the skis.

"Hit it!" I yell.

The boat roars forward,
the tow line snaps tight.
I leap from the water,
riding the waves.
"Lean back!" they scream.
How much? I think,
then smack the water
like an angry northern pike.
I fall three times—
a flip, a somersault, the splits.
"Want to try again?" they ask.
Papa skims the silver water
on only one ski.
"Yes!" I shout.

Up north at the cabin,

I am always brave—

even in the dark woods,

when blood thumps through my head

like old Ojibway drums.

It's said they beat for two full moons

when Chief Ma-kwa's son

rode to the sugar bush

but never came home.

I stand and listen

and think I hear them still.

Up north at the cabin,

we are almost ready to go.

I check under my bed,

take down our clothesline,

pack my snorkel and fins.

Then one last thing:

I look all around me—

at the screen porch,

at the creaky branch I hear at night,

at the chipmunk hole under the stoop,

at the tufted island in the bay,

at the spot in the sky

where the North Star shines.

I shut my eyes tight

and fix them in my mind.

So when I'm far away from summer,
when frosted windows cloud the sun,
I close my eyes
and once again
I am up north at the cabin.

MARSHA WILSON CHALL spent her childhood summers on northern lakes, but the real inspiration for this book came when she returned to the north woods with her own children. "Watching them embrace nature, revel in their imaginations, find a freedom they simply do not have in the city, is a radiant experience year after year," she says. "My daughter always cries when we leave."

Ms. Chall lives with her husband and their two children in Minnetonka, Minnesota. This is her first book.

STEVE JOHNSON and LOU FANCHER have collaborated on four children's books. Each has stirred memories of their childhoods. Mr. Johnson spent many summers fishing in lakes so clear that he could see smallmouth bass swimming near the dock. Ms. Fancher remembers sharing peanuts with chipmunks and steering a red motor boat.

Mr. Johnson and Ms. Fancher are married and live near several lakes in Minneapolis.